to Jodie

Chapter 1

O N MY THIRD day in Oregon, I leave my motel
room, get breakfast at a diner, and call home. My
mom says that she made sure that my doctor forwarded
all my medications from North Carolina to a CVS phar-
macy nearby. She wishes me luck and reminds me that I
have an appointment in an hour. After crossing town, I
park and walk into the therapist's office nestled behind
a big fern across the hall from a dermatologist office,
shuffle some insurance papers around and have a seat. It's
raining outside, and I take a deep breath to prepare me
for this next big step in my life. A spectacled lady with
short, professionally-gelled hair and a relaxed smile comes
out and introduces herself as. Dr. Chandler. We walk
back to the cozy, pillow-strewn therapy room complete
with cinnamon aroma candles, and she says, "Well, I

would like to start out today by you telling me a little bit about what's going on. Tell me as much as you feel comfortable with. Start with what you were feeling when you became ill the last time and then fill in as much of your story as you can so that we can work together on this. I'll just let you talk it out today, and we'll start a dialogue next week. Are you ready?"

"Ready," I say. In my mind, I had the following monologue running in my head as it had been for a couple of weeks: *I suffer from bipolar disorder. On that day, it was like a sparkler burning and exploding in an orgy of red light dancing to the laughs and shouts of all those around. The light slowly flickered out. Then, there was total darkness until the next one was lit. This back and forth continued until the last sparkler went out. The darkness was all-consuming, like a blanket wrapped way too tightly around me on a cold winter's night. The restraints of illness started to wrap me as I gasped for air. My hands were shaking, and a general sense of panic set in. Memories flashed before my eyes, but none of them seemed to help me find the path. Those thoughts and memories were hopelessly out of order anyway.*

Somehow, the night turned to pitch black, and I couldn't find my way back to the path. If only I had brought my flashlight or my phone with me to help light the way. I went through the woods, scraping my legs occasionally on the thorn bushes below me. No one else would have understood even if I tried to explain what was happening to me. I finally found the country house, closed the screen door behind me, and collapsed on my bed for another night of fitful sleep.

That night was some months after the start of that terrible, exhilarating, unbelievable summer, but my story really began in 1977 when the weirdest kid in town came into the world. Instead, I simply say, "Maybe I should just start from the beginning with my story."

I was born a dreamer in the small town of Gastonia, North Carolina. I was the middle child of a doctor and school teacher, and everything seemed to be idyllic in our little world. There a swing set in the backyard and a playground within walking distance. I was absolutely carefree as a child, and I had a wild imagination. Often, I would turn down play dates, preferring to play by myself, and my mom didn't think anything of it since I was thoroughly entertained. I would run and climb trees with the greatest of ease, but around company, I was painfully shy to the point of being almost mute. At five, I went to the neighbor's house and back to ask for sugar without saying a word. That's how quiet I was among grown-ups. Even so, I ran with the neighbor kids just fine because together we would occupy an incredible imaginary world that would take us on boat trips in my uncle's disabled Bay Cruiser sitting in the backyard and to other unheard of places.

Things started to change the summer before first grade. I needed glasses, and I was fitted with a huge brown pair that would prove the bane of my existence.

My sheltered world was starting to crumble. First grade started at a very small private school boding ill enough, but midway through the first semester, the teasing stared in earnest. I made friends, and I even had a group with whom I rode bikes to school. The school was so small and the part of town so elite that these were to be my friends for a few years at least, and we regularly met in front of Jones' corner store to ride bikes together to school. However, my own friends couldn't help but tease me at times, and I had little choice but to make myself comfortable in my personal hell of childhood's cruelties. My mother was there to catch me through all this, but at such a tender age, I had no way to know that her battle with alcohol was making us into emotional co-dependents for life. My sister could see my mom drunkenly arranging mine and my brother's lunches at night, but I wouldn't be exposed to this ugly truth until middle school, when it could hurt the most. Even so, my mom would try to play tough, telling me numerous times to stop being so sensitive, but I was too often overcome by the feeling that I did not belong.

In my pre-teen brain, I thought that my appearance could change my reality. After five full years of getting four-eyes taunts, I finally reinvented myself by getting contacts, but this small improvement didn't really change things. I was not excluded from things, but I felt lost in the crowd. I felt that I was invisible to girls, I struggled at sports, and my self-esteem suffered as a result. My parents did their best to help me, but I was just a melancholy little kid. They would try to reason with me, and my mom was always there to console me when the neighborhood kids would make fun of me during late afternoon games of four-square. I think they perpetually thought my unhappiness was part of passing phases of my growing up. To further set me apart, I had taken up acting lessons and had gotten a part in a local theater production. Acting was a great thrill for me, but it further isolated me from my peers, and it really brought out my eccentric side. Ultimately, all I really wanted was my parents' affirmation, but their response was lukewarm at best. They were kept very busy by my older sister's drama that saw her taken out of my school due to bullying and into an all-girls school where the atmosphere was equally tough. I'd want to blame my brother who was just one grade below me at the same school as well. I think that three kids was one too many for my parents, and it's all too easy for us middle children to get lost in the shuffle. Through it all, our greatest times as a family were out on the boat, fishing until sunset and of course, drinking. The photos document that the adults were always drinking. I would find out later that both my father's parents were hard drinkers, partying drunks you might say. However, my mom's father was a hardened AA veteran, and her chances of living though a party lifestyle unscathed were very slim. My emotional state which was so intertwined with my mother as a shy first grader on the four square court would collide with her heavier drinking states growing up.

Fifth and sixth grade passed by, and I tumbled from the frying pan into the fire. My school only went up to the eighth grade, but the elite prep school across town was K-12. As she so often did, my mom made an executive decision with my future and moved me to the new school so that I would have a sure place to continue through high school. For the first semester, I really withdrew into my shell, but I did play football, which helped me meet people. I hadn't gotten any more athletic, but I liked being part of the team. Still, the specter of alcoholism was ever present. My brother moved schools in the same year, and he had his spend-the-night party crashed by my drunk mom just coming to check on them. He was mortified, and I too lived in fear that everyone at school would know that my mom was a drunk, as if that meant there was something wrong with me.

I took guitar lessons from Frank Rissuto downtown. I had been very quiet about this interest, but the new school meant a new opportunity to showcase my talent. Music became my obsession as I started to hit puberty. I started playing the guitar, and I soon found a few guys at school that played too. We got a garage band going. This project stretched from the height of the Guns-n-Roses era in into the grunge period with Nirvana and Pearl Jam, and we rocked out "My Michelle" and "Smells Like Teen Spirit" for the whole neighborhood to hear.

This was fun, but my real interest was music from the sixties from the Allman Brothers to Dylan to Cream and Hendrix. My mom had been in the peace movement in the late sixties, and I wanted to recreate that era in my mind in order to understand what she might have experienced. The problem with all this was that I didn't really have much musical talent beyond the basic chords progressions. Still, it was fun except for regular fist fights with our drummer, who insisted on picking on me at every chance.

Playing in a rock band was something to do, but at this high school it made us the brunt of older kids' taunts more than their cheers because all the older kids were pretty much stuck on finding their best track to Princeton Law than dreaming of a record contract. At public school, we would have been a hit, but not so much a private school. The real emphasis was on official extra-curricular activities, the kind you can put on a college application. So I felt pressure to play three sports a year in middle school, whether I wanted to or not. I wasn't very good at any of them, but my dad seemed to think that he was doing his fatherly duty by showing up for games. We weren't close. To make matters worse, his partnership was dissolving, and he spent way more time at the office and especially at the hospital than he did at home. That left my mom in charge, and she just couldn't handle it but spent a lot of time bragging about my sister's amazing academic exploits as if they were her own.

I felt a lot of pressure to succeed academically on top of sports and everything else, and something just gave way.

Things started to really deteriorate as I started to experiment with drinking and pot. At parties, I would numb myself, and it shielded me from the social interaction that I really needed. It was around that time that I started to discover the extent of my mother's drinking problem, and in a cruel twist of fate, I dulled the pain of this family illness with more drinking and drugs. It was rather like pouring gasoline on the fire and then adding some firecrackers to the mix, but I didn't care. My dad, meanwhile, was too busy delivering babies at all hours of the night to notice the dumpster fire that his home life had become. My sister in her senior year was as rebellious as ever, and shouting matches between her and my dad were the stuff of legend around the block. These conflicts only fueled my resolve to do whatever I wanted under the radar, thus avoiding the fights and confrontations with my parents. Despite all this chaos, all three of us children got great grades, and that seemed to excuse everything.

College came sooner that I would have thought, and I continued my drunken, overachieving ways at a small liberal arts college, Williamson College, in South Carolina. Being a frat boy with a 4.0 seemed to be the ideal, but it was an illusion for most. I could keep up with the books and with the drinking, but I didn't connect with my classmates very well. I did try to socialize, but

I had a lot of anxiety making it difficult for my social skills to improve much. However, I did make some good friends in my fraternity, and I hoped that these friends would help me on down the road. I felt lost through four years, including a stint studying abroad and backpacking through Europe. I really thought that my studies were my ticket to a great career and life. I was really driven by a genuine intellectual curiosity, but it was a fear of failure that drove me as I pushed on through to graduate school with my diploma in hand but all sorts of problems unresolved. Something had to give, but I couldn't see it at the time.

Midway through graduate school, it all hit the fan in slow motion. I was a twenty-four- year-old graduate student just finishing up a year-long paid internship in Stockholm. The winter was rough on me, but generous quantities of vodka at parties helped me endure. Much to my family's surprise, I took up cross-country skiing so that the grey winter didn't overpower me. Still, I wasn't much of an athlete, but I tried my best to keep up with a membership in a university ski club. We enjoyed a weekly ski every Sunday exploring the rolling country-side. On one occasion, I even joined the group for an afternoon at the sauna. I reluctantly agreed to broiling in the sauna followed by a mad dash to immerse myself in the snow. Then we ran back to the sauna to warm up. That thrill was unmatched in my whole stay in that beautiful, frozen country.

Carl, my best friend in college, and I had been planning a train trip across Europe for three years. Since the fall of the Berlin Wall, the whole map of Europe was open to exploring, and we wanted to take in as much of it as we could. I met Carl in Amsterdam, and we spent two days having a look around there, not forgetting to take the Heineken factory tour. On our first train journey, we set off at night towards Berlin. I wanted to take in the museums, but Carl naturally preferred the beer gardens. I won out, telling Carl that there would be plenty of time for beer gardens once we got to Munich. We both really enjoyed the Berlin Wall museum, which chronicled the many escape attempts East Berliners tried over the years to escape to West Berlin and freedom. After a fine three-day stint in Munich,. Prague was the next destination on the trip. Prague was definitely my favorite place I'd seen so far. I loved the old town with its huge clock overlooking the square. I also marveled at its amazing bridges. On the tour of the castle and the surrounding area, we saw the odd little house where Kafka once lived. Carl, an English major in college, informed the crowd that this area was the setting for Kafka's novel *The Castle*.

The pace slowed some as we pulled into Budapest and set off to enjoy the view from the old city, Buda, down to Pest, where the magnificent whitewashed walls of the Parliament building could be seen across the Danube River. The remarkable thing about Budapest was that the local people paid no notice of us being "rude" Americans. The locals could have cared less, and it was frankly a relief after meeting more Americans than locals in the last cities we visited. We stayed almost a week, and we even took a side trip north to take in a local wine festival. The Europe trip concluded with a long train trip to Nice for a few days on the beach. Then, we hit Paris and caught all the high spots. Lastly, we headed back to Amsterdam for two days before flying back to the States. This trip sure was a whirlwind tour of Europe, but it was worth every penny. We went our separate ways in New York, promising to stay in touch via Skype and to share our photos on Facebook.

After arriving back home safely in Gastonia, I started to realize that I hadn't really stopped my breakneck speed since arriving in Stockholm almost a year ago. I felt reinvigorated. Since I had six weeks until school started back, I looked for things to keep myself busy. My parent's house was very quiet since they had left for a year-long sabbatical in Australia. In my quest to keep busy, I rode his bike twice daily, volunteered at a soup kitchen, and read as many novels as I could get my hands on. I even started toying with ideas for my thesis, which wasn't due until next spring. In my remaining free time, I cleaned the house three times over, and I read the *New York Times*, the *Wall Street Journal* and the *Charlotte Observer* almost daily. I took particular delight in phoning friends from graduate school to regale them with stories of my trip. To put it bluntly, I was in overdrive.

The one speed bump to the end of my summer came when I met my sister and her family for a week at the Carolinian Mountain Resort. We didn't call it a resort. It was more like a family camp, really. My sister and her friend from high school brought their whole families up for the week. They all marveled at just how active I was. I was riding my bike that I hadn't touched last summer. I was going on hikes before breakfast and was fully participating in all the activities. The old me would have remained on the porch, quietly reading books for most of the week. They also couldn't get over how thin I was. They started calling me "the new Jim." There, my sister invited me to Brevard for the next weekend. She said that it must lonely all by myself in that big house.

Before heading for Brevard, I drove back to Gastonia to pick up the mail and to check in on things there. As I was about to head out the door, I noticed the voicemail light blinking on the home phone. There was a woman's voice on the tape that I didn't recognize. It seemed that the call was from the university, and they said that it was urgent. I immediately called the university to find out what was so pressing, and my call was forwarded to the financial aid department. While on hold, my thoughts raced to figure out what the financial aid office wanted. When a lady finally picked up, she said that due to recent budget cuts, my grant had been eliminated. She said that she was sorry, but I needed to pay all the tuition costs for the coming semester by next Tuesday. I dropped the phone and stood in shock for a moment. Then, I went into panic mode. I called my sister in Brevard to ask for her advice, but she said that I'm speaking so fast that she couldn't understand me. I struggled to tell her that I would see her in Brevard in a few hours. I checked the clock and figured out that it was impossible to call Australia at that hour. So, I left for Brevard with a million thoughts running through my head. How would I get the money so quickly? What if Mom and Dad couldn't afford to help me out? Was there a way to stall for time with the bursar's office? These were all reasonable questions. Instead of thinking through them rationally, my mind swirled like a tornado tossing each new thought into the melee in my head.

I started off to Brevard in my powder blue Volkswagen station wagon. My mind continued to race from one thought to another, but this battle somehow did not affect my driving. Even so, I surprisingly failed to turn on the air conditioning and didn't once turn on the radio. By the time I reached my sister's house, I was covered in sweat, and I felt like I could have thrown up at any moment. A long car ride usually helped calm me down. However, my nerves were frayed by the thought of not being able to finish my studies. My whole life plan hinged on getting my degree, and I could feel the chance slipping away.

I waited outside my sister's house for fifteen minutes and left two voice mails on her phone. I felt too agitated to wait any longer, so I took my bike off the car rack and went for a ride. The immediate neighborhood was familiar to me, but I got lost after I unwittingly crossed a major intersection and went into another neighborhood entirely. I tried to backtrack, but I only got more lost. I finally went into to a store where they kindly let me use the phone. Thank God my brother-in-law was home, and after a puzzling conversation, he agreed to meet me at a local supermarket. I sat down on the curb outside the supermarket, and my brother-in-law, Todd, arrived in his trusty old Suburban. We threw the bicycle in the back and headed back to their house. I felt so embarrassed that I didn't say a word until we pulled in the driveway.

As I stepped out the car, I was bombarded by my sister screaming, "What the hell do you think you're doing?" I stared blankly ahead and rushed past her and up the stairs into the safety of the upstairs bathroom. Ever since having her first child, my sister's fuse had become very short. I was already afraid of what she might say next. I dried my eyes and proceeded slowly down the stairs. Instead of being mad, she was perfectly calm. She just pleaded with me to tell her what was wrong. I responded that it was nothing to worry about. She pressed me again for information, and I responded by collapsing in the nearest chair and crying.

I explained my situation through intermittent sobbing, and she assured me that everything could be worked out. I replied that if only I hadn't taken that trip, then everything would have been worked out by the time the new semester rolled around. I was insistent that all the blame lie on me for this mixed-up situation. I pushed myself up from the lounge chair and started mumbling incoherently about all the stuff that I had done to ruin my life. I was convinced that all I did now would just work out for the worst. My sister tried to console me, but she couldn't stop me from pacing long enough to make me listen. I collapsed in the chair and started sobbing again. My sister went into the next room to call her friend who was a nurse, and luckily she was at home. She told my sister to take me to the hospital where they would probably just give me some medicine to calm my nerves. There was an eerie quiet in the car, and I realized that my whole body was shaking after a few minutes in the car. I saw my sister's sense of concern on her face, so I shut my eyes to make the ride go easier. On the second half of the ride, she talked to me very calmly, assuring me that the doctors at the hospital could help me and that I didn't have to go if I didn't want to. She made the experience sound almost nice, but when we got to the hospital, it was a different story.

Before we got out of the car, I came out of my dream-like state and realized where I was. I begged to go back to the house. I said that everything would be just fine if I just got some sleep. In Gastonia, I had been getting about four hours of sleep per night. We got there at six, but we had to wait for fifteen minutes for our turn.

I could feel the clock ticking in my head, and the wait seemed interminable. I started shaking again as I thought about the possibility that they might ship me somewhere where I couldn't escape. The nurses interviewed my sister first, and then they called me back to the consultation room. I tried to play it cool, but my rapid speech and shaking hands gave me away. Apparently, my sister had successfully convinced the nurses to consider admitting into inpatient care, which meant that I would likely be there are a while. I wasn't really with it enough to protest coherently and thus began my first experience with the mental health system. The orderly took my belt and all my personal effects for safe keeping. My sister filled out some more paperwork, and I sat down in the wheelchair as directed. My sister kissed my cheek and waved good-bye promising to be back tomorrow to visit. The orderly turned the key to open the big metal door, and I glanced behind me as the door slammed shut, maybe forever.

My vision got fuzzy as I looked up to the ceiling where the off-white incandescent bulbs seemed to burn my retinas. I was wheeled to my Spartan room with two metal bedframes and twin nightstands where I was told to change into hospital clothes. So, that was it - I was officially in prison, and when the jailer shut my door, I felt like it was a cell door slamming shut, and the off-white color of the walls must have matched my face at that moment. I felt sick. I could see by some shirts on the bureau that I had a roommate, and this revelation makes me more nervous.

I then walked down the hall to find the TV on the Golf Channel, which served as background noise for all the thinking I had to do. The rec room had dirty dark red carpet, and there were two younger ladies and an older gentleman sitting in wicker chairs seeming to follow the action on the screen, I just kept on thinking, My rumination was soon interrupted by the announcement of dinner, and I went through the buffet line. I sat at an empty table and looked down at the unappetizing mix of Salisbury steak, mashed potatoes and some unidentifiable mix of greens. The meal wasn't bad, but I barely touched my plate. I was still angry at my sister for flinging me into this place. I went down the hall to my room to lay down for a bit. I got up when someone knocked on my door and told me that we had a chance to go outside into the courtyard. Most of the other patients were smoking, so I kept my distance. I couldn't wait to meet some of my fellow inmates tomorrow. After outside time, a line formed to parcel out our meds, and I had no choice but to take them. Now, I was remembering that there had been a doctor in the room earlier, but I couldn't remember his name. That's who instructed me to take this awful pills that made my head feel like a corkscrew was going through it. I crawled into bed and fell asleep long before my roommate slid into his own bed. The lights in the hall never went out, and I wasn't allowed to close the door, but I slept some anyway.

I felt groggy the next morning at breakfast. My roommate who was a black-haired, rough-skinned man in his late forties, slid into a seat across from me. He said with a smile that I must have considered myself lucky that I wasn't scalped the night before. I found the comment strange and alarming, but he explained that it was a joke. He was half Native-American. Next, there was an hour-long information session where I got to meet some of my fellow patients. First, there was Carla, who claimed that her family put her there to keep her quiet about some drug running scheme they were hatching. There was a big woman named Yolanda who wound up in there every time she missed taking her medication for more than a day. When it was my turn, I said emphatically that I should be at the university by now instead of sitting in this hellhole. "Activities" such as group exercises on goal setting and meditation practice continued throughout the day, and it seemed that the only thing we couldn't do was leave or lie in our beds all day.

My sister and her husband came to visit at four, and she watched Todd and I play a few games of ping pong. My sister surely sensed how bitter and upset I was with her, so she stayed silent for most of the visit. They asked if there was anything that they could bring for me. I just wanted her to bring the Book of Common Prayer. It is said that inmates often find God in their new environment, and I wanted to give it a try. I didn't want to cause a scene between myself and my older sister because I wanted to get out as soon as possible. Before dinner, I met with the doctor. He reintroduced himself as Dr. Johnson, and I nodded politely. He asked me a series of questions about what was happening in the world, what I did that day and how I was feeling on the new medication. Finally, I just got up the courage to ask what's wrong with me. He said that the preliminary diagnosis was schizophrenia or maybe bipolar disorder. Neither sounded good, and I wanted to escape this awful place as soon as humanly possible.

The next day trickled by. The only good news I got was that my roommate was leaving, so I would have the room all to myself. The family visit was even more bitter and silent than the past one. They did bring the prayer book, but the nurses wouldn't allow me to keep it because it had a string for a place marker that could have been used to hang a rat I supposed. After our visit, I started planning my getaway. I succeeded in duping the nurse by not taking my pills that night or the next morning.

Five in the afternoon was the time the time I had set for my escape. It seemed like the prefect time between the hospital's and my sister's schedules to minimize the chance of something getting in my way. Truth was that I could have left whenever, but my mind had fixed itself on a very specific plan, and I was going to stick to it. During the doctor's daily rounds, he recommended that

I stayed four more days at least. So, I would leave against doctor's orders, but I didn't care. My sister would arrive in a few hours for visiting hours and find me gone, but the thought of her reaction didn't stop me. I had to get to where I could sort things out on my own. At exactly 5 pm, I signed a few forms, collected my belongings and sat down to check what was in the bag. I retrieved my wallet and heard my keys jingling at the bottom of the bag. It was a miracle that my sister hadn't taken my keys. Now, freedom was only a taxi ride away. Off I went with a fifty in my pocket for the cab ride.

I nearly tumbled out of the car when we reached my sister's house, and in another thirty seconds I sped out of the neighborhood. Luckily, no one ran outside to stop me. I hit every green light out of Brevard. At one point, I topped ninety as the speed rush coursed through my veins. That terrible place hadn't sucked all the life out of me after all. I made Gastonia in record time, and the first thing I did when I got home was raid my parent's liquor cabinet. The next thing I did was kick my feet up and watch Sports Center on the big-screen TV.. After about five cocktails, I started to feel woozy. I also felt a little bit guilty about what I had done. So, I texted my sister, "Sorry. Thanks for trying to help me, but I just had to get out." One drink later, I passed out on the couch.

I woke up at eleven the next morning, and I realized that I couldn't stay at my parent's house because my sister would know where to find me. I also figured that drinking every night by myself would get old fast. So, I called one of my wildest college buddies to see if I could crash for a few nights at his place. Unlike most of my college friends, Tim didn't want a real job. He tended bar in downtown Charlotte and partied after hours at least three nights a week. By a stroke of luck, I caught him just before he went to work, and he said that he was happy to have me stay. I screened my calls all day until it was time to leave for Charlotte. In a rare moment of clarity, I parked my car outside Tim's apartment and walked to the LYNX station. I arrived at the bar around 9:30, and Tim greeted me with a bear hug. He bought me a beer and a few shots, and since it was a slow night, his boss lets him go just before midnight. Tim insisted that we hit a club or two before heading home. The strobe lights and pulsating music made me feel like I was hallucinating, so I excused myself to go outside and get some air. After chilling out for fifteen minutes, Tim came outside to check on me. Tim asked me how it was going and got a muffled "not so great" in response, so he drove us back to his apartment. I rallied, and we stayed up until three in the morning drinking beers and reminiscing about college life.

Since Tim didn't have to work the next night, he planned on having a little party. His two roommates were still in college at UNC Charlotte, so the party promised to be a lot of fun. While Tim got ready for the party, I took LYNX downtown. I checked out two museums, and I had a nice late lunch at a café in the heart of the financial district. The towering skyscrapers made me feel pretty small, being hungover in the big city, but I did find a nice little park to sit for while away from the late afternoon bustle. I was grateful for this escape from my troubles, but I couldn't help but feel a little depressed wandering the streets of the Queen City all alone. I got back to the apartment just as the pizzas were being delivered, and I inhaled two or three slices right then, knowing that I would need something in my stomach for later. Probably forty or fifty people showed up, and I downed a beer and realized that I was not sleeping that night. When I told people that I was in grad school, they seemed impressed. However, I knew that it was a lie. Now, I was a bum living in my parents' empty house. I stayed by Tim for most of the night, and I genuinely enjoyed meeting so many bright-eyed college students. At three-thirty in the morning, I brushed several beer cans off the couch and crashed on the make-shift bed. I was still sleeping at eleven when Tim woke me. I leapt out of bed and wondered where I was. All I wanted right then was a nice warm bed. After changing into some clean clothes, I thanked Tim for the hospitality but said I must get back home to Gastonia. Tim tried to persuade me to stay one more night but to no avail.

As I headed toward Gastonia, my mind started racing again. I wondered what my sister might have done in my absence. What if there were people out looking for me? What if my sister called Mom to come back from Australia to take care of me? These questions were simply too much for me to handle right then, so I cranked up the radio and enjoyed the ride. Once I got home, I slept for twenty-four hours straight, only getting up to fix some cereal and to go back to bed. Like a dark cloak over me, depression set in.

I couldn't count the ways my life had potentially changed in the past week from grad student to mental patient. I just wanted to wind back the clock to before I got sick. After sleeping so long, at about two in the afternoon, I rose from the bed, pulled back the curtains and felt the sun coming in through the window. After a little rifling through my closet, I found a pair of jeans and a t-shirt that fit me. I felt a little dizzy after a full night and day of hibernation. I went to the bathroom and splashed some water on my face. Then, I took a nice long, hot shower, and I felt refreshed. However, the shower didn't stop my mind from racing. So, I concentrated on fixing myself a nice, hot meal. There were still frozen chicken breasts and vegetables in the freezer. I just concentrated on one thing at a time like they told me to do at the hospital.

As I washed the dishes, the phone rang from across the room. I ran over and saw that it was my sister calling. I had a clear choice to make: to either pick up the phone and go along with whatever my sister had decided for me or to let the machine pick it up and keep going on my own. I picked up the phone. My sister said that she had talked to Mom, and they had decided what to do. All I got to say was "uh-huh" to everything she said. A few hours later, I heard a car honk outside, grabbed my bag and got in my sister's car. We were headed on the seven-thirty flight to Baltimore.

I barely noticed my surroundings until we were about to land. My sister unbuckled my seatbelt for me and led me to the exit. I only had one small suitcase, not nearly enough for my stay, but she said that she would mail me some more. We caught a cab outside the airport, and we sped into downtown Baltimore. We could have been anywhere as far as I was concerned. Getting out at our destination, I looked up a towering building, and we went inside. I sat for two hours idly as my sister met with the intake officers of the hospital. The place was not on our insurance, so my parents were having to agree to pay a portion of their retirement savings so that I could be treated at such a world-class facility. Later, they would say that I was worth it, but I sometimes wonder if a potential villa in Hawaii would have convinced them to have spent their money differently. Once the papers were signed, I had to go upstairs. That's when the anxiety kicked back in. I said goodbye to my sister once again, but she promised to fly in for a visit in three weeks. When every hour produced a different reality for me, three weeks seemed like a lifetime.

And it was. Life in the hospital was a world unto itself. Gone were the scary dayroom and suicide checks.

The rooms were spacious, the food was good, and the doctors were top notch. I had my own personal nurse that met with me for an hour every day! She had gone to Yale! I knew I was in good hands. I was no longer afraid, but I was still confused. Panic about the future dominated my waking hours, and I began to think back to my undergrad days in History class and hatch conspiracy theories out of thin air. It wasn't bad enough that my scholarship was gone, but the world was collapsing in on itself as well. I would later learn that this was what is referred to as dissociation. The doctors adjusted my meds almost daily, but I didn't really know the difference. I do remember that a team of three would come into the room every morning to talk to me, take notes on their clipboards and look pensively at me and at each other.

Mealtime was the real chance to talk on a personal level with fellow patients. Notice I say patients instead of prisoners because human dignity was really valued in such an expensive facility. I sat with the same group every day, but different types of patients had different assigned eating areas. For example, the eating disorder patients were only allowed to sit with each other, I guess because they had dietary restrictions. It was at lunch one day that I befriended Greg who had freaked out after watching the coverage of Hurricane Katrina for four straight days and wound up in the hospital. Yup, that would do it. More structured conversations were had in group twice a day, and we would lay out a future world for ourselves that we all knew was never going to happen. However, the counselor made everyone feel good for a while. We went downstairs to the gym to play basketball for an hour every day. This was fun, but I didn't exactly have enough energy to play a full court game or anything.

I missed seeing my family. My sister was in North Carolina, and my parents were overseas. The countdown to my sister's visit began. Two days before the visit, I spent three hours in the rec room making the perfect card for my nephew, Stephen, who was coming with my sister to see me. My nephew was only two, and his photos brightened up many nights studying for me in grad school.

Finally the day arrived, and I lit up. My sister came though those doors with my nephew by her side, and I hugged her tight. She met with the doctors for a few minutes and then signed me out at the front desk. I was allowed to go out under her supervision into Baltimore for five hours. We caught a cab to the harbor area. The Baltimore area had really been cleaned up in the past few years, and it sported nice views and a restaurant and shopping area that was really quite appealing. Mainly, I wanted seafood. We got a table, and once we got my nephew settled, I decided on the shrimp and crab special. You can't go to Baltimore without trying the crabs, and they weren't serving any in the hospital. I was nervous about the time, but my sister told me to relax and enjoy my food. After the meal, we wandered down where there was a dock overlooking the harbor. My sister convinced me to go with my nephew on a paddle boat ride. Only the paddle boat was in the shape of a purple and green dinosaur. As medicated as I was I at the time, I will never forget it. Even so, the visit was bittersweet.

My sister and nephew left that afternoon, and I still had three weeks left. Things did get better, and I gradually I was allowed more freedom. I remember that they would take us for walks around the part of downtown Baltimore near the hospital. I recall wondering what those old brownstone buildings must have witnessed over the years. As nice as Baltimore was, I wanted to go home. The doctor visits got less frequent toward the end, but I had to fill out a lot of paperwork and some surveys for a study that the university was conducting. On the second to last day, it came: my diagnosis. Bipolar (not schizophrenia as the county hospital had suggested). I would hold onto this word like an identity badge for some time to come, but ultimately, it's just code in a file along my journey through life. Those life lessons would come much later. Now, I had to fly home with my sister and face the immediate future.

My sister came to pick me up, and this time, I was crying tears of joy. The road back wasn't easy, but it was better than the alternative. There were ups and downs but not like before. On the plane ride back, I asked to sit in the window seat so that I could see down from the heavens to the green grass and the occasional Target with its red bull's-eye painted on the roof. My parents got back from Australia in time for the holidays, and I got set up in a studio apartment across town with intentions of finding employment soon. Following doctor's orders from here on, my life slowly got better. I landed a nine-to-five job. It was entry level, but I couldn't be too picky at this stage. A month later, I struggled through a crippling eight-day period of depression that nearly got me fired. Trying to cheer me up, my sister invited me along for a weekend at the country house. My depression followed me there, but being around family helped a little. I inched ahead by constantly finding things that I enjoyed and by concentrating on them to help me through the weeks and months ahead. The big finale of my next summer was my nephew and godson's third birthday party. I circled the day on my calendar, and I busied myself with finding the perfect gift. The day finally arrived, and I pulled up to my sister's house in that same powder blue station wagon. I set my present down on the table, and my nephew ran up to give me a big hug. The look on my nephew's face as they cut the cake was and would stay crystal clear in my memory like a talisman to ward off all the evil in the world. However, as with any lifelong illness, the struggle wasn't over.

Two months later, I felt really good, and the weather was beautiful. I had more energy than I ever had before. I decided to go the country house by myself this time just to get away. I was running through the woods. Memories of childhood bullies kept running through my mind. I couldn't make it stop. Then, blacked out scenes from parties started popping in my head. I remembered that legal pad with my plan for college written out on it, and I collapsed. Nothing made sense anymore, and I felt like I was doomed. I was sick again. I didn't wind up in the hospital this time. My parents had come home by then, and I was able to stay with them until I could decide what to do. The decision was made that I had to get out of North Carolina. There simply weren't enough resources there to adequately deal with my situation. All my options were dead ends, and I needed something innovative and new to help me escape my demons and to face life with a renewed vigor that simply wasn't possible in my current surroundings. Heading west, I felt lost, hopeful and afraid.

The therapist interrupts: "That's all we have time for today. Let's start back there next week." She says, "Thanks for sharing." I feel a cathartic wave come over me as I get up from the couch. I walk slowly out the office to my car, get in, and drive to my motel. Luckily, it's my last night. I didn't drive all the way to Oregon to this particular therapist. I have come for a farm wellness program designed to prepare me to re-enter regular life with skills that their staff are trained to provide. The farm is said to provide a great atmosphere for this healing to occur. I move to the farm hostel tomorrow, and I can't wait. The job sounds great, and I am so thankful for everyone who made this move happen. As of tomorrow, I will working on a farm run by a non-profit. I will be getting the help I need to sort out all my childhood issues. The stress that so plagued me before will replaced by the clean rhythm of farm life, and I will be surrounded by friends in similar situations. This will be my new family. I will always remember my family back home in North Carolina, my college friends and all the experiences that defined my former life. However, the call of the wide open fields, the river nearby, and the 6 a.m. wake-up bell will compel me to move on the best I can to fulfill what God put me on this earth to do: seek peace and harmony in the company of others while working to build a better tomorrow for all. My old demons will always haunt me, but the rush of the river will help wash them away.

Chapter 2

I PULL THROUGH THE gates on the outskirts of town the next morning. My car is full of stuff for the trip, but I would only really need a fraction of it for my stay. The brochure says that the conditions would be Spartan, and as Cathy, the center's receptionist, points out on our little tour, the rooms have twin bunk beds. The dining area and rec room are nice though, and as an added bonus there's no TV. There's an election coming up soon, and the last thing I want to worry about is who the next leader of the free world will be. I set my stuff down in room number three, at which point, I am set free to roam about the grounds and get to know the place. I walk over a bridge overlooking a lake and a big green field with a herd of cows in the distance. To the left, there were several barns, and I could see several residents hurrying around doing various morning chores. I almost make it to the frontage road when I hear a voice calling me back. It is time for my very first co-op meeting.

I expect a hippie commune-type feel, but the leader, Phil, is quite businesslike. There are fourteen of us in all, seven men and seven women. Apparently that number would fluctuate periodically. I am introduced first as I grin sheepishly in front of the group. The rest call out their names, but my mind can't keep it all in. I wonder almost aloud what all their stories must be, but I am stopped short by the slide show demonstrating the new milking machine. This is really happening. Never in my life did I see myself as a farmer, but here I am in this little slice of paradise tucked into rural Oregon.

I am spared 5:30 milking duty the next morning, but just after breakfast, I am sent to feed the chickens with Max from Atlanta. He was in the bunk across from me the previous night, but we didn't get a chance to talk. He had been a meat manager at a supermarket before bipolar illness and alcoholism had sent his life careening off a cliff. He has more tattoos than anyone I've seen to date, including one of a female body part on his shaved head. I certainly wouldn't have met this guy in a grad school class, but he was very nice and committed to the program.I could see that it wouldn't be too long before he would be back in Atlanta showing that town how it's done.

Routine is the mainstay of farm life, but without regular breaks, we would lose it. So, we organize games of kickball in the field, and with each passing afternoon, my stamina grows. We also are absolutely fanatical about our food. Farm fresh, obviously, and everyone plays a role in ensuring the highest level of nutrition. Poor diet and poor mental health are strongly correlated, so this holistic approach to health for both mind and body is essential to our collective wellbeing. Going back out into the world without all the essential lifeskills is considered pointless, and our leader stresses that the process starts with what we put in our bodies. After ten days, I start to feel rejuvenated in a good way, and it's time to head back in town for my second therapy session.

Dr. Carson greets me cordially, and I have a seat. She says that I seem a little stressed, so that maybe we should start with a five-minute meditation. My voice still a little shaky, I start, "So where do you want us to start?"

She replies, "Well, we will get to some underlying issues later, but I'd like to start with you telling me about your sources of strength. It seems that your sister plays a big role in your life. Why don't you tell me about her?"

"Sure," I say. "She has always been my idol, my protector. She always had the most thoughtful gifts for me growing up. A faux leather jacket like the one Tom Cruise wore in *Top Gun* and a cassette player that ate up every new tape she collected. I followed behind her in every successive musical obsession from the Beach Boys to the Beatles on up to REM. At times, I looked up to her too much. She smoked and drank at an early age, so naturally, I thought it was cool. My sister was my listening ear for all my future plans, only I sensed later that she wasn't really listening and wasn't really qualified to give good advice anyway. Still, I adored her, but I also feared her. She got a 1450 on the SATs and got into every college she could have wanted to go to. She was a tough act to follow, and I didn't feel up to it. Still, my parents expected excellence from their children, and I had to buckle down and get with the program."

The therapist says, "You talked a lot about your sister in the first session. What was her role in your initial recovery?"

"She was patient. I don't think that she knew what was really going on, but she was my advocate in any case. I described the visitation at the county hospital as pretty antagonistic, but I failed to mention what she brought without me asking. She brought me a beloved children's book like a subtle reminder to keep things simple. The in-house therapist said that my sister was pretty saavy. When I got back from Baltimore, she hired a local girl to be my personal attendant. We did chores by an Excel spreadsheet and even took trips to the local library and the park. I was pretty irritable and hard to live with, but she grinned and bore it. I am not sure what it did to her husband, but he seemed to take it in stride. She always had a place for me at her home, and I was glad to be included. Her kids felt like my kids really, since with my life nearly wrecked, I wasn't really planning on having any of my own. I guess you would say that because I am the middle child, I hold onto my nuclear family a little too tightly. My sister sends me daily emails here even though she's pregnant again and busy running her own business. Looking up at her, life always seemed so easy, but I didn't know how much she really had to struggle in her own life too. I guess I idealize my family in my mind."

The therapist says, "That is very common for a person in your situation. But here, we're going to be working on you dealing with your present reality. I don't want you to forget about your family inasmuch as they give you strength, but your life on the farm has to be simplified and purposeful. Do you understand?"

"Yes," I say with a tear in my eye. "I guess I just miss them is all.

The therapist hands me a tissue. "Of course you do," she says. "However, I want you to focus on the present moment, and just try to get through each day here moving one step forward. Let's try another meditation, and I want you to envision your ideal life on the farm."

The music starts playing, and I drift off a bit. I picture a 6 a.m. dip in the lake, waking totally refreshed and ready for breakfast. I parcel out the food for others before grabbing my own plate, and we eat quickly as there is work to be done. We have to chase a chicken to take it back to the egg-laying area. There's laughter all around. Work continues unabated throughout the day, and we have time for our daily game of volleyball. After dinner, we sit around a fire while someone strums a guitar, and we soon drift away back to our beds for peaceful sleep. I can't remember the last peaceful night's sleep I got in North Carolina.

Coming back to consciousness, I tell the therapist what I had envisioned.

She says, "That's great. I think we've made a lot of progress here today. Just remember to put your best foot forward on the farm, and I am sure things will continue to get better for you. See you next week."

Chapter 3

I PULL INTO THE driveway feeling the cool air on my arm through the open window. Scanning the open field, I see a girl beside the well crying. I park quickly and walk over to see what's the matter. I ask what's wrong, and she looks up and says, "I'm finished."

"Surely that can't be true. You're young. You'll be okay." Her name's Emily, and she's twenty, but she didn't look a day over seventeen.

She says, "You don't understand. My family has given up on me, and if I don't make it out of this place in one piece, I may never see them again. Then again, that may be better because my dad doesn't believe that there's anything wrong anyway."

I reply empathetically, "I am sure he's just concerned about you, even if he might not really understand what's going on."

She goes on, "You see, I was in college, and everything was fun and I was having a good time. Then, second semester came along, and the classes got really hard, and I tried to buckle down and get good grades, but no amount of concentrating would give me results I had gotten in high school. I caved in and started to party and stay up until all hours Monday through Thursday writing paper after paper. Finals came around, and I lost it."

"What happened?" I say.

"My roommate came in while I was studying and listening to music and threw a fit that my clothes were all over the floor. I snapped and threw a shoe at her. She lunged at me and missed as I went rushing out the door, and I slept on the grounds outside the quad that night. There was a drum circle going nearby, so I wasn't totally alone with my rage and fear for the coming exam at 8 a.m.. It was safe to assume that I would flunk the exam, and I made a D. My roommate had reported me to the administration, and I had to go to counseling or be kicked out of school."

"What happened then?" I say.

"Well, my dad made me stay for summer school because he didn't want to see me at home and because I had to make up my one failed course. Counseling continued that summer, but the guy was a total boring jerk.

I was hungover during most of the sessions anyway. Fall semester came around, and they made me go see a doctor. They claimed I had bipolar disorder. I was allowed to take a reduced class load, but my dad threatened to cut me off. My mom tried to intervene, but it was only by a court order that my dad continued to support me. He didn't believe that mental illness was real, at least not for me. The pressure got too much, and I started sleeping around. I didn't take the medicine for a month and got drunk most nights, but I could still do okay in the two classes I was taking. It was only after getting busted by the cops for public drunkenness in the alley beside a bar downtown that my dad got serious, sobered me up, then sent me here."

"After all that, I'd say you're pretty lucky to be in a safe place like this, and rest assured that everybody here knows exactly where you're coming from." I say.

She replies holding back a sob, "I just feel like my future's ruined."

I reply, "No, you're just changing course. I'm sure good things will happen for you if you let them."

Suddenly, my problems didn't seem so huge. I patted her on the shoulders and said. "Come on. I'll make us some green tea, and we can join the others for dinner prep."

She says, "Tea sounds nice. Let's go."

Chapter 4

I HAVE DISH WASHING duty tonight, so I am stinky and sweaty as I sneak into the back of the rec room for the evening movie. The movie is educational this time. The two previous nights, they had shown cheesy Hollywood movies. I had skipped those to write emails back east and to do work in my diary. I am sure that the documentary / educational film will be boring and that I will get more writing done real soon. But the director says that we aren't allowed to leave, and my face starts to contort into a growl as the movie starts. The film is called *The New Normal*, and it starts in with some catchy music and some really cool cityscapes. It continues with a series of interviews from real people who have successfully adjusted to life after their diagnosis. It all starts with an honest self-assessment followed by the process of finding your place in society. Most of them were doing very different things from when they got the diagnosis, but they seemed happy. Diet, exercise, and effective scheduling were also stressed. All the things that we do every day on the farm but seem so hard in the real world. After twenty-five minutes of the film lecturing me, a woman came on the screen that crystalized the message. She said that every moment awake will constitute your battle against mental illness, but every moment will be worth it, as she held up a picture of her two kids. So, there really is a new normal, even if I have no idea what it is yet. I fall asleep that night with an image of that woman's kids in my mind while wondering what my sister's kids are up to. Mercifully, I sleep soundly through the night.

Just before dawn, six of us gather by the lake for mediation practice. Breathing in and out the mist by the lake alleviates the pressure and worry that would accompany future planning meetings with the counselor that afternoon. Our breathing just about synchs up when we hear the breakfast bell ring. There's no manic rush to our morning routine. We are challenged to enjoy every bite of our omelets and fruit. I smile throughout the meal for the first time in living memory. Jokes are exchanged with the passing of the bread, and an encouraging pat is given to a new girl still feeling down. It's together that we can cope, so that in the not-too-distant future our new-found strength will carry with us to wherever we land.

My sense of tranquility is interrupted though when I go back to my room to find that my journal is missing and my CDs are spread out all over the other bed. My first instinct is to start cursing and panic.

I try not to yell, but George, one of the counselors, hears me anyway. He says, "Calm down. We can work through this."

I breathe heavily and say, "Why can't these guys just leave my stuff alone?"

"I'll get him back here to clean this up right away, but we need to find a way to calm you down." He calls outside to another counselor, "Hey Justin, go get Travis, his roommate, over here to clean this up." Then, he says to me, "Just breathe and tell me what's really going on."

"This just reminds me too much of how my brother used to rifle through my things without ever asking. I never said anything to him because he was a foot taller than me and would have beat me up. I just can't escape these situations. I'll always be the one that gets run over."

He says, "You know that's not true. But we're going to fix this and do it calmly."

I say, "How do I forget what's been already done to me?"

He says, "You don't, but you will get better at managing every day, I promise, but you have to work hard at it and keep a positive outlook. Positivity is key. Now here comes your roommate to clean everything up and apologize." I watched him clean up the stuff, we shake hands, and I start to feel better.

Leaving the dorms, we both walk out into the field where the group is assigned the daily tasks. I work with Alice and Jennifer for the morning. They're both from California. They both worked in Silicon Valley with really amazing high-pressure jobs in the tech industry. They had been at the farm longer than I had, and at this point, they both seem to be at peace with it. We take turns milking the cows, and I am amazed at how at ease I am around these girls. Multitasking is discouraged at the farm, but sloth and inactivity isn't. I am tired by lunch break, and we've filled up eighteen jugs so far. I go by the office to take my medicine, and I start to feel more at ease as the benzodiapines start to kick in. This stuff is a street drug on the outside, but my doctor says the medication properly managed will help me sleep and cope better. What's really been helping me cope better is talking to all these interesting people here, and I feel like I could write a book about them by the time we are done, but there's a confidentiality clause in the admissions process, kind of like at an AA meeting. Oh well, I think what I have to say in my counseling sessions would more than fill up a book, and like clockwork, another one rolls around on Tuesday of the next week.

Chapter 5

I FIND A NEW app on my phone that gives me anxiety reducing meditations, and I really needed them today because my therapist was running forty-five minutes late. She had to run to her kid's school to pick him up sick and rush him to the doctor's before starting my session, the first one after the lunch hour. I wonder how a person could teach people how to be less stressed if they had such stress in their own lives. The thing about the farm and Oregon is that it's easy to smile in those situations, and my iPhone is a life-saver with its meditation apps. She doesn't skip a beat as she walks in the door and calmly invites me back to her office as coolly as she had the first time we had met. She offers me some tea, and this time I take some green stuff with lemon. I need to stay calm for what I'm about to go over.

The therapist notices that I walked in looking dejected with bad posture, and she suggested that we start with some breathing exercises. Just past twenty breaths, she says, "Okay, I think we can start now."

I tear up but start in anyway. "Alcoholism ruined my childhood. I also knew that my mom was my idol. We had the same interests: sports, history, and foreign language, but I felt from a young age that I carried the weight of all the expectations that family, alcohol, and circumstance robbed her of. As a young child, I never knew that there was a problem, but my sister did. I halfway wish she had clued me in earlier, but that wasn't to be. All I knew is there was a lot of yelling in the house, but I never really knew why.

When I did find out at twelve that she drank too much, I could only weep inside watching her with her drink beside her, reading trash novels until midnight and watching Sportscenter. There was no way she could go back to teaching the way her drinking was. She tried to go back to school to get credits for certification, but the pressure exceeded her reading ability and coping skills. As a last resort, she learned to do insurance for my dad's office, and depending on her binges, she would show up at the office between 10 and 12 every other day if they were lucky.

I alone felt sorry for her, and a lot of good it did me. Co-dependency is rough, and considering that my siblings took after my dad, they had only a little trouble separating themselves from my mother. I don't want to make it sound like it didn't bother them, but they were just able to be a bit less conflicted later on. I learned at a party in high school the hard way that you never bring up the fact that your parent has a drinking problem to people you don't know very well. I carried around a lot of hurt at school as well, and it didn't help that people were mean to me and that I had few close friends. I can remember seeing an ad for Jim Beam on TV one day and having the uncontrollable urge to go to Kentucky and burn down the factory. But I was back to drinking beer on Friday night.

I learned to rationalize early, and I thought that beer was okay but that liquor was absolutely off-limits. The whole small-town Southern Episcopalian scene in our town glorified drinking as the lubricant of upper-middle-class society, and it made me mad and powerless at the same time. The worst thing was my dad's attitude. He drank, but he couldn't be an alcoholic and a doctor, so that problem was solved. But he was absolutely fatalistic about my mom's drinking. His parents were alcoholics later in life, and he considered it to be his lot in life to live with alcoholics. What I could see clearer than anyone was that my dad was an asshole and treated my mom poorly, but because my siblings took after my dad, they didn't blame my dad. It takes more energy to be mad at both of them and to be trapped between two clones of my father for most of my childhood.

Then, there's the question of whether or not I was an alcoholic. I don't think so, but I stuffed my emotions a lot by drinking. I just wanted to know why my mother drank so much so that I could do something to make it all right. Once in college, she came to pick me up, and she stonewalled me for an hour and a half refusing to utter a word about why she drank so much. She had the unique ability to clam up on topics that she didn't want to address. I spent Bid Day at my fraternity drowning my sorrows rather than having fun. At that age, I did a lot of things out of a sense of duty, and drinking was one of them. I look back now see all the waste that alcohol has caused. It kills joy and replaces it with hurt, sarcasm, and nostalgia. I longed for my early childhood when everything was great, but I can't ever get back those wonderful playtimes splashing in my grandparent's pool."

The therapist interrupts, "This was a lot to process. Is your Mom still drinking now?"

"Yes." I reply. "But less than before."

She says, "You understand it's a disease. Like you have bipolar, she has alcoholism. It's going to be a struggle for both of you, but you can make it. Now I want you to pick up some literature about being the adult child of an alcoholic on your way out. We'll talk about some of it next time. Believe me, you're not the only one out there going through the exact same thing. You will find comfort in knowing that eventually. Just remember, this isn't your fault. Now, why don't we close with a meditation. Would like some more tea?"

"Sure" I say.

We drift off in a trance-like state, and before I know it, I'm pulling back up to the farm with a smile on my face.

Chapter 6

THE NEXT TWO weeks at the farm are busy. We get a new sheepdog, Rex, as both a therapy dog and as a pet for the director. Everyone loves that dog, and he is very playful and affectionate. We take turns at evening program snuggling up next to him, and everything seems okay when you snuggle up to his belly. I also make friends with the chickens that I have to tend to every morning, and I discover that they each have their own unique personalities. I'm not saying that they're smart or anything, but they are lovable. The geese are a different story. They poop everywhere and serve no discernable purpose.

The daily chores start to build to the point that I don't even notice that another month has gone by. Therapy meetings more and more focus on my immediate future than my past, and here in Oregon, things seems hopeful. However, I have no family support system here in Oregon, so I am probably going to have to go back to North Carolina to live with my sister for a while until I get settled. I will miss the fresh air and the camaraderie, but I am also hoping that there is a normal life out there for me somewhere.

On a Friday, I go into town to get a full tune-up on my car because I am heading back across the country in a week. I am going to stop in Denver on the way back because my aunt just moved there, but the rest of the trip will be pretty lonely. That afternoon, I scour the thrift stores to find used audiobooks to listen to so that I am not alone with my thoughts for the whole ride back east. I sit up by the lake until 3 a.m. the night before I leave just to soak in the cool air and inner peace that I've found here. May it carry with me to a saner reality.

I don't look back pulling out of the gates, and before I know it, I'm at my aunt's table in Denver enjoying a home-cooked meal. She doesn't have much news to relay except a little bit about what her son's up to in Montana. I thank her for the hospitality and head off for a very boring drive.

I pull into my sister's driveway, and no one is home. I just sit in my car listening to my audio book until she pulls in behind me. We hug, and I get my stuff out of the back of the car. Inside, she tells me that my mom has arranged a therapist visit for next week and job interview for the week after that. I get this sneeking suspicion that I am going to need to find a job out of state soon because having my overbearing mom control everything in my life is just not what Oregon set me up to do.

Then, after dinner and after my sister's kids are in bed, I find out what is really going on. My mom's drinking has gotten much worse. My sister's just glad that I was off in Oregon while it escalated. They're not sure what to do. We spend the next few days walking on eggshells. I talk to my mom twice on the phone, and she seems okay to me.

Things come to a head the next Tuesday when my cousin Susie in Atlanta gets a strange, friendly call from my mom at 7 a.m.. She is calling to chat about some trivial family business, only she was drinking for the past twenty-four hours, and she thought that it was 7 p.m.. After Susie gets off the phone with my mom, she calls my brother in Charlotte and sets the wheels in motion for staging an intervention. About ten friends and family are notified to attend, and we find an interventionist, Mr. George Stone, from Charlotte, who comes highly recommended throughout the whole process. At this point, my recommended "as-needed" anxiety meds go up to three a day, and my sister wonders if it's even a good idea for me to attend the intervention. I decide to do it anyway, and in a few days I'm on my way to Gastonia to do my part.

I pull up to the IHOP just outside Gastonia and see my aunt Cindy waiting in the parking lot. She's my dad's sister, and she doesn't have to be here. I'm glad she is because she has always been nice to me. We talk about Oregon for ten minutes, and I start to feel so wrapped up in my own issues that I almost forget why I'm here. The intervention. Several more relatives and close friends arrive so we can all get our marching orders from Helen. After much build-up, she simply goes over the secrecy of the whole thing and the schedule for the rehearsal next Monday followed by the actual intervention the following day. My mom's good friend Rachel is letting us use her house for it, and the whole thing hinges on a proposed bridge game between old friends, some of whom rarely see each other anymore. The pancakes are delicious, and I feel oddly at ease listening to old stories among relatives until it's time to head home to sit out an especially anxious week.

The next Monday comes. I find myself sitting in a fold-out chair in Rachel's living room listening to Mr. Stone's white-board lecture on the progressive disease of alcoholism. It's not new information, but his delivery drives home its seriousness. He says that the intervention has to create a bottom for my mom where the only way out is to get help. At the break, I find myself wondering if I reached my bottom and gotten the help I needed in Oregon. I can't wonder long because after the break, we assemble to practice the intervention in two rounds: the statement and the consequences. In the statements, everyone says how we were hurt by her drinking, and during the consequences, we say what will happen if she doesn't get help. At that point, any number of scenarios seem possible, and I'm so nervous that I don't sleep that night.

The next day, I park two blocks away and walk to the house. She can't be allowed to see familiar vehicles in the vicinity and be tipped off. Everyone is there. Her college roommate from New Jersey arrived three hours ago just to do her part. We are ready, but I start to feel queasy. I remembered to bring my medicine bag, so I take an anxiety pill and a Mylanta with a big glass of water. I go over my prepared lines in my head until the door opens. My mom sweeps a glance of recognition over the whole room before dropping her head. Standing by the door next to her, Rachel says, "Ann. Listen. We just want to talk to you." She grabs my mom's hand and gently walks her over to the one empty chair. My mom doesn't say a word. She spent decades perfecting a stone-cold expression that never let her emotions show, and even now, her face doesn't flinch. Mr. Stone says to her, "You'll have your turn at the end, but first, these people have something that they'd like to say."

My sister starts. "Mom, I couldn't bear to see you stumbling around while preparing lunches for my brothers at night when they were little. I couldn't bring my girlfriends to spend the night in middle school because I was too embarrassed. But that doesn't matter now. I have kids. What am I going to tell them when you are always repeating yourself? That their grandma's a drunk? Mom, please get help. I want my mother back."

Her old roommate, Margaret, says, "Ann, you really hurt me when I came down for Run Gastonia, and you were too hung over to watch me compete. I showed up at your house afterward, and you were just making breakfast at 11:30. Please get help. I want my friend back."

My father clears his throat and says, "Love, I hate to see you like this. All those nights I carried you home from dinner parties hurt me. Alcohol has destroyed too much of your talent and ability. You know I want the best for us. Please get help."

It's my turn, and I choke up. I can't handle it. I just manage to say, "Please get help, Mom. I don't want to be embarrassed to have you as a mother anymore. Please get help."

The testimonies go on, and I start to feel a bit dizzy. Everyone just wants her to get help and feels that this is long overdue. Through it all, my mom is utterly still. I desperately want to know what she's thinking, but she's a steel trap. After the statements, Mr. Stone offers her a chance to get help by travelling in my brother's waiting car to the treatment center. She stays bolted to her chair.

Mr. Stone says, "Now, everyone will have the chance to share what will happen next if you choose to keep drinking." We start from a different side of the room, and Uncle Ted says, "If you don't get help, we won't see much of each other anymore, I'm afraid."

A weak beginning compared to my father's powerful and utterly resigned consequence. He says, "If you don't get help, we won't have much time left together." He wouldn't leave her. Co-dependency has been his life, but it still leaves him near tears.

I think that my mom is starting to crack through the next two consequences, but it took my sister's to finally do it.

She looks my mother right in the eyes and says, "Mom, if you don't get help, you won't ever see your grandkids again." The effect is like a bomb going off in the living room. Stunned silence fills the room, and all eyes turn to my mother. In exactly five seconds. My mom lifts her head, nods and says simply, "Okay." She walks out the door followed by my bother, the chauffeur.

Chapter 7

THE NEXT TIME I see my mother she's out of rehab and sober. She says she's ready to put the past behind her. If only I am not so wrapped up in the past. Part of me is back in Oregon doing breathing exercises and part of me is flashing back to my early childhood at my grandfather's pool swimming after my mother's raft. Happiness and joy mix with relief and anxiety because it's not over. Living with bipolar is a daily struggle, and I have to get started, ready or not. I start to look for a job in Brevard. I find one shelving books at the local library. It's part-time, but it gets me out of the house. I also start studying and reading in my free time. If I wasn't really good at managing my affairs, I was always good at school. Weeks turned into months, and I added another part-time job and got a place in Brevard. Everything felt so up in the air, but tenuous felt better than free-fall. I didn't need to take the GRE because my scores were still good from before.

However, I am adjusting my expectations greatly. I have decided to become a librarian, and I won't even have to leave Brevard to do it. There's an online course through UNC-Greensboro, and I arrange to work part-time as a library assistant in Brevard while I complete my two-year degree. I won't ever make a lot of money or equal the success of my siblings, but I think it will make me happy. My new therapist is thrilled for me, but we still have a lot of work to do with dealing with fear, anxiety, and interpersonal skills. At this point, it all seems overwhelming, but being close to my sister makes a big difference because I know I always have support.

Two years later, I walk at the graduation ceremony in Greensboro, and three months later, I get a librarian job in Greenville, South Carolina that proves very challenging due to the work environment. However, two years later, a job opens up in Fayetteville, North Carolina that's a perfect fit for now, and I breathe a sigh of relief that my life has achieved a moment of peace. In my free time, I start taking some creative writing classes like I've always wanted to do, and I see my sister's kids as often as possible. I know that meds and treatment are my reality now, but life has so much more to offer that I ever thought possible on my first day in the hospital and that even nightmares can have happy endings.

CPSIA information can be obtained
at www.ICGtesting.com
Printed in the USA
LVOW13s1316171017
552742LV00016B/65/P